Jonah's Trash...
God's Treasure

Published in Nashville, Tennessee, by Tommy Nelson™, a division of Thomas Nelson, Inc.

Library of Congress Cataloging-in-Publication Data
Anderson, Joel.
    Jonah's trash--God's treasure / written and illustrated by Joel Anderson and Abe Goolsby.
       p. cm.
    Summary: A simple rhyming version of the Bible story in which Jonah has to be swallowed by a
big fish and more before he learns to respect the commands of the Lord.
      ISBN 0-8499-5825-3
      1. Jonah (Biblical prophet)--Juvenile literature. 2. Bible. O.T. Jonah--Biography--Juvenile literature.
3. Bible stories, English--O.T. Jonah. [1. Jonah (Biblical prophet) 2. Bible stories.--O.T.] I. Goolsby, Abe. II. Title.
BS580.J55A53 1998
224'.9209505--dc21

                                                             97-32655
                                                                CIP
                                                                AC

Printed in the United States of America

98 99 00 01 02 RRD 9 8 7 6 5 4 3 2 1

Jonah's Trash... God's Treasure

by Joel Anderson

Illustrations by Joel Anderson and Abe Goolsby

Photography by David Bailey

Thomas Nelson, Inc.

Nashville

"Mr. Grungy is my junkyard name. Storytelling is my greatest pleasure.
My trinkets will tell a tale of truth. One man's junk is another man's treasure!"

A prophet is a man of God who speaks a message from above.
God spoke to the prophet Jonah, giving him a message of His love.

Trash & Treasure Hunt
Find four coins.
Count the spools for thread.
Read the hidden word.
Find the odd card (it is red.)

God said, "Take a boat to Nineveh. Tell the people they don't have long.
In forty days I'll destroy their city if they don't stop doing wrong."

But Jonah said, "I don't like those people. I won't do what You say."
So he got on board another ship that was heading the other way.

Trash & Treasure Hunt
Find seventeen fish
and two oysters with pearls.
Hunt for six kinds of food
and things which gross-out
some boys and girls.

5

The boat set sail, and Jonah thought, *I'll hide from God on this trip.*
But God was watching Jonah sleep down in the bottom of the ship.

6

Trash & Treasure Hunt
Find six things to eat
and twelve bottle caps.
Find part of a telephone
and something which SNAPS!

7

So God whipped up a mighty storm, and the sailors were filled with fright.
They bowed to all their worthless gods and prayed with all their might.

Trash & Treasure Hunt
Find three pencils,
fifteen shells,
three kinds of string or cord,
and something which smells.

Trash & Treasure Hunt

Count the clothespins.

Find three animals running free.

Look really hard to find six light bulbs.

Add up the dice (they are less than twenty).

The sailors woke up Jonah and cried, "Start praying to your God, too!"
But he knew the storm was all his fault, so he told them what to do.

"God sent this storm to stop me. I've been running from the Lord.
The only way to save yourselves is to throw me overboard."

The sailors threw Jonah overboard, and the raging storm died down.
As Jonah sank down in the chilly sea, he feared that he would drown.

Trash & Treasure Hunt

Count the cereal on the ship.

Find a clothespin and twenty-four fish.

Find two pencils, two watchbands,

and a handle which makes water swish.

But God sent a mighty fish for Jonah with a huge mouth opened wide.
The great fish swallowed Jonah whole and kept him safe inside.

For three long days and three long nights, Jonah prayed inside the fish,
"Lord, I'm sorry I ran away from You. I'll do anything You wish!"

KETCHUP

SIN WILL KETCHUP TO YOU!

Toothpaste

CHOCOLATE MILK VITAMIN D
Purity
Purity
CHOCOLATE MILK VITAMIN D

INSTAMATIC II

Trash & Treasure Hunt

Find a pair of glasses
and six things you can eat or drink.
Find something which after brushing,
you spit into the sink.

So God made the fish go to Nineveh, where it spit Jonah on the shore. God said, "Jonah, tell the people not to do evil things anymore."

Trash & Treasure Hunt

Count the pinecones
and the shells washed up on the shore.
Find at least ten metal things
and something which unlocks a door.

17

Jonah preached to the Ninevites, "Change now or you will die!"
The king and all the Ninevites began to pray to God and cry.

Trash & Treasure Hunt

Find something sweet, something salty, something which flies, but is not a bird. Find a bug swatter and four screws, and read the hidden word.

19

But Jonah was upset with God. He said, "Lord, this isn't fair! This city was full of evil people. Now good people are everywhere!"

Trash & Treasure Hunt
Find five pencils and three nuts,
three screws and a spring.
Count ten royal cookies
and a tipped-over dog thing.

So Jonah sat down in the blazing sun, hoping Nineveh would burn.
God said, "Why are you angry, Jonah? When will you ever learn?"

Trash & Treasure Hunt
Find twenty-one pieces of candy,
a penny, and a clock for your arm.
Read the hidden message.
Find five animals from a farm.

God sent a vine to grow over Jonah to shade his roasting cap.
Jonah liked the cool shade it gave, and he took a little nap.

Then God sent a worm to eat the vine. And the vine shriveled in the heat.
Now Jonah was mad and burning hot, from his head down to his feet.

Trash & Treasure Hunt

Find twenty-three marbles, a pencil,
and two things which get very hot.
Read the hidden word.
Find the animal who likes to trot.

"I'm so hot and I'm so mad. And Nineveh is just fine."
God said, "I wish you loved these people as much as you loved your vine."

So Jonah learned a very big lesson, much to his displeasure...
the people who he thought were trash were really God's great treasure.

Trash & Treasure Hunt

Find eight buttons, four coins,
and five things for eating corn.
Find ten light bulbs, three screws,
hidden treasure and a golden horn.

27

Trash & Treasure Hunt

Find two sailors and Jonah,
and the men who made this book.
Find the rope, the fish, the king,
and a worm with a hungry look.

The End